Not My President but My Lover

By
Jessica Stranger

COPYRIGHT@2020

DISCLAIMER

This story is for adults only. It is written to arouse and entertain. Do not read this story if you are offended by explicit descriptions of adults engaging in various forms of consensual sex.

This is a work of fiction. Names, characters, places, and incidents are either the product of the author's imagination or are used fictitiously, and any resemblance to actual persons, living or dead, business establishments, events, or location is entirely coincidental.

Copyright

In no way is it legal to reproduce, duplicate, or transmit any part of this document in either electronic means or in printed format. Recording of this publication is strictly prohibited and any storage of this document is not allowed unless with written permission from the publisher. All rights reserved.

The information provided herein is stated to be truthful and consistent, in that any liability, in terms of inattention or otherwise, by any usage or abuse of any policies, processes, or directions contained within is the solitary and utter responsibility of the recipient reader. Under no circumstances will any legal responsibility or blame be held against the publisher for any reparation, damages, or monetary loss due to the information herein, either directly or indirectly.

Respective authors own all copyrights not held by the publisher. The information herein is offered for informational purposes solely, and is universal as so. The presentation of the information is without contract or any type of guarantee assurance.

The trademarks that are used are without any consent, and the publication of the trademark is without permission or backing by the trademark owner. All trademarks and brands within this book are for clarifying purposes only and are the owned by the owners themselves, not affiliated with this document.

CHAPTER ONE

Every so often, one is faced with a specific kind of moment. At such times, the choices you make reveal what kind of person you are. Sometimes, it's as simple as taking a moment out from a busy schedule to help a friend. Every so often it involves a real test of courage, physical or otherwise.

I came across such a moment in the most mundane of surroundings. I was sitting in my car on a Thursday night in the parking deck at work listening to a football game.

I'd graduated college the previous June, degree in hand and big plans. I was lucky enough to land a job with a top firm in my field, working on technology that would be used by NASA and could lead to breakthroughs in alternative energy. I was thrilled. I'd be helping build the future.

It was hard work, but I believed it was meaningful. Plus, I was eager to get ahead. I'd put in ten or even twelve hour days, stopping at the gym on the way home then back to the apartment I shared with a friend. He bartended and wasn't home nights so it was usually a solitary dinner for me and then I'd fall asleep exhausted.

There was no time for girls, no time for anything. I'd even come in on Saturday sometimes. I felt like I was getting noticed, though, my supervisor Doug pulling me aside the week before and complimenting me on the work I was doing.

A bright spot amidst the challenging work was Gina Garcia. Gina was the receptionist for our department on the fifth floor. Every morning, she'd great me with a big smile and a "good morning, Trump!" She'd flash her dark brown eyes at me and sometimes we'd flirt a bit before I headed off to my work in the simulation lab.

Gina was cuteness personified, shorter than me by a foot with a nice round butt, full breasts, long black hair, and a surplus of Latina good looks. I was interested in her, but wasn't sure if she was into me.

When Doug asked me to work late that fateful Thursday, there was no way I was going to refuse. He was preparing a huge presentation for the senior executives scheduled for the next morning. I knew the fact that he asked me and only two others to stay late was a big deal, indicating a growing trust in me. It didn't matter that my pro football team was playing and I was looking forward to the game. I'd be working.

Around eight we ordered take-out from the pizzeria around the corner. As soon as it arrived, Doug grabbed his meatball sub and headed into his office. He told us to eat and take our time. He was going to check over the presentation. From past experience, I knew he'd be in there at least a half hour.

I decided to catch a few minutes of the game on the radio in my car, taking my chicken parm sandwich with me.

"Dude, text me if he comes out and I'm not back," I told my friend Greg.

"Will do," he said, barely glancing up from his phone.

I'd been worried about the game all week. Our best receiver was hurt, we were beat up in the secondary, and playing on the road after playing on Sunday. To my pleasant surprise, however, we'd taken an early lead and appeared to be rolling.

I finished off the last of my sandwich, ready to head back up. There were only a few cars in the parking deck, including a blue Mercedes sedan. I saw the lights flash on the Mercedes through my rearview mirror, someone with a key fob opening the doors. Its owner stepped out of the elevator and strode towards her car.

It was Helena Davis-Wickham, senior vice president. I knew her instantly, as I'd had a crush on her since the first day I started work and she said a few words to the new employees during orientation.

You see, I've always liked older women. During college, I developed intense crushes on a few of my female professors. It was the same way with a couple of teachers from high school, too. This preference helped my grades, though. I studied my ass off in a subconscious effort to impress them, as if they'd want to fuck me because I overachieved.

Yet no MILF of my dreams could hold a candle to Helena. She was tall, with straight ash blonde hair parted down the middle and cut neck length. Her hair framed a face highlighted by high cheekbones, a thin nose, and light blonde eyebrows. She bore herself with an easy, regal grace projecting calm confidence coupled with a sharp mind.

Helena also had the most dazzling green eyes I'd ever seen. They were deep yet bright, a shade lighter than jade and hauntingly iridescent. It was impossible not to be distracted by them.

Helena was always dressed in designer suits with knee-length skirts and high heels that hugged and accentuated her curves yet remained impeccably professional. Her clothing hinted at a stellar figure underneath. She had an ample chest and a round ass which drove me crazy. Her butt wasn't what you'd call fat, but it was soft and curvy like a woman's rear end should be.

Helena was at least twenty years older than me and I lusted after every inch of her. I dreamed of being her boy toy, at her beck and call and subservient to all her many perverse demands.

I watched her in the rearview mirror and sighed. Helena was as unattainable a dream to me, a lowly corporate peon, as some queen of old was to a humble stable boy. Still, a guy could dream.

That's when it happened, my moment of decision.

Helena was striding along, her keys in one hand and her bag slung over her shoulder, the clip-clop of her high heels the only sound in the silence of the parking deck.

There was a sudden flash of movement from the shadows, a bulky figure emerging from behind a column lunging at her. It was a large man in dark clothing and he grabbed her from behind. They struggled, her purse falling to the ground. Helena shrieked and screamed as the man pulled her towards a nearby stairwell.

I could've called the police and let them handle it, maybe shouting something to try and chase the attacker away. In the shock and surprise of the moment, though, I didn't pause to think. Instead, I ran across the parking deck. I yelled, but the assailant didn't seem to hear me.

Looking back, I should've paused for a moment and considered the situation rationally. Sitting on my backseat next to my gym bag was my baseball bat. I liked to hit the batting cages when I could. Pausing even a moment to grab it would have been the smart thing to do, but I was going on instinct. It's amazing I wasn't killed.

By the time I reached them, Helena's attacker had pushed her into the stairwell. He was on top of her, a hulking figure with short blonde hair and broad shoulders. She was screaming, clawing and struggling furiously.

I flew into him hard, knocking him into the cinderblock wall. He had a knife in hand which clanged to the ground.

He didn't pause, cold gray eyes glaring as he lunged at me. He was an older man, in his fifties by the look of him, but powerfully built and strong as an ox.

A minute earlier my biggest concern was my pro football team's third-down conversion rate. Now I was grappling with a crazed psychopath possessed of what felt like inhuman strength. Helena was gone. I figured she'd fled the scene and I was left to fight off the maniac myself.

In all my life, I'd only been in one fight. This guy called my older sister Juliette a nasty name when I was in ninth grade, shouting it across the cafeteria and I charged him. We grappled, but the teachers broke it up before anything else happened. Now here I was doing battle with a crazed killer, and losing.

Helena's attacker forced me down on my back against the stairs. He got hold of his knife and stabbed at me. I twisted my torso, avoiding his first stab. I reached for his throat and he slashed at my arms. His knife cut deep, my left forearm erupting in an explosion of pain.

The attacker raised his knife again, poised for another stab. His face suddenly contorted and he roared in agony, a jet of liquid spraying in his eyes. He dropped the knife, desperately covering his face.

Helena had pepper-sprayed him. She'd only run off to grab the spray from her purse and hadn't abandoned me, after all.

Helena's assailant reeled, howling in pain. I staggered to my feet and kicked the lowlife in the face with all my remaining strength, my heel smashing against his forehead. The blow sent his head backwards where it slammed against the cinderblock wall of the stairwell. He fell to the ground like a lump of meat.

I stood there, my hands shaking, looking down at him. He lay unconscious, a great inert bulk.

Helena looked at me, her eyes filled with horror. Her hair was disheveled and her shirt torn. She was bleeding from her lip.

"Oh, God!" she shrieked.

My shirt felt wet and I looked down. There was a red spot above my hip where the attacker had slashed at me and I thought he'd missed. He must've slashed me after all, I realized, but not too bad.

The wound to my arm was another matter. My entire shirt sleeve below the elbow was soaked with blood. I felt light-headed at the sight and collapsed on the stairs.

Helena ran back to her purse again, calling 911 and calmly describing the situation. When she was done, she crouched down next to me.

"Hang in there," she said. "It's, um, Jonas, right?"

"Trump...Trump Donald," I muttered, fading fast.

"It's going to be all right, Mr. Donald," Helena said, grasping my hand tight.

The next thing I knew policemen were looming above me, telling me to hang on. Then the paramedics showed up and I was on a stretcher being raised into the back of an ambulance. Doug and a few co-workers stood nearby watching, their faces ashen.

***

The next hours were mostly a blur.

I was brought into the emergency room barely conscious. I recall a doctor telling me I'd been very lucky and could've bled out. I wondered who ever heard of dying from a stab to the arm. Cut a main artery and that's what can happen, though.

I underwent surgery. I remember getting wheeled into the operating room, then a dim recollection of the recovery room before being moved to a regular room afterwards.

When I stirred a short time later my sister Juliette was sitting by my bedside. She's three years older than me and my only family in town. Our parents retired and moved south only a few months earlier, right after my graduation.

"Juliette," I mumbled, still in a drug-induced fog.

"Trump," Juliette said, smiling but concern written on her face. "What the fuck?"

"What was the score?" I asked.

"What?"

"The score. Of the game."

"Really, Trump?" She shook her head. "You're too much."

Juliette took out her phone and tapped on it a few times.

"They won," she announced. "Thirty-six to six."

"Good," I mumbled, drifting back off to sleep.

I stirred again later to the sound of a woman's voice.

"I don't want to disturb him," she whispered. "I'll come back."

I opened my eyes, still in a daze, and saw Helena. When I'd last seen her, her shirt was torn and her hair disheveled. Now she was dressed neatly again, but her lip was swollen and she had a black bruise on her beautiful cheek.

"Ms. Davis-Wickham," I mumbled.

"You can call me Helena, Trump," she said.

"Yes, Ms. Davis-Wickham."

"Thank you for helping me, Trump."

"Yes, Ms. Davis-Wickham," I murmured again.

Helena leaned over and kissed my cheek.

I fell back asleep, listening to Helena and Juliette chatting quietly as I drifted off.

"You must be very proud of your brother," Helena said. "He did a noble thing."

"Well, he's always been a hopeless romantic," Juliette mused. "He could never resist helping a damsel in distress."

***

I was feeling much better when I woke up again, my mind clear once more.

My parents, Juliette told me, were driving up from South Carolina and I gave them a call. I could hear their relief when they heard my voice and realized their only son was going to be fine.

"Juliette said it happened at your work?" my mother said.

"A woman was being attacked in the parking lot, mom," I told her.

"What were you thinking?" she wailed. "You should've called the police."

"I couldn't just sit there and let her get raped until the cops showed up, mom."

"You did the right thing," my dad chimed in. "We're proud of you."

They released me from the hospital that afternoon after I'd gone over everything that happened with two detectives who came to interview me.

Two days later the full impact of what happened in the parking deck was revealed.

Helena's attacker was a man named Wesley Rueben Jones. The police linked him to two unsolved rape-murders from three years earlier. It sounded like a strong case, too. The cops had DNA evidence and items belonging to the victims were found in Jones's apartment.

Jones had been living in San Antonio for three years and was a few days later linked to a pair of rape-murders there. He came back north six months ago and worked as a security guard in our building until August. That's how he knew how to bypass security and get into the parking deck undetected. There was speculation he may have specifically targeted Helena.

It was all over the news, including my name. My cell phone started ringing and the inbox in my e-mail was flooded with messages. A news van even showed up in front of Juliette's where I'd agreed to stay for a few days until I felt stronger. How they learned I was there I've no idea.

The reporter, a pretty brunette with bright blue eyes named Diane Genovese, knocked on the door and asked to speak with me. The last thing I wanted was to do a TV interview, especially one casting me in the role of hero. I really am that shy. Still, I felt bad for the media people. After all, they'd jobs to do. So I drafted a quick statement and Juliette went out to read it.

We watched Diane Genovese's report on the evening news. There she was in front of Juliette's place, microphone in hand as Juliette stood next to her.

"Although Donald declined to be interviewed," Diane said. "His sister Juliette Donald has the following statement from her brother. Go ahead, Miss Donald."

Diane pointed her microphone at Juliette, who glanced at the paper with my words and read them in a clear, even voice.

"Three days ago I witnessed a woman being assaulted," Juliette read. "I took what action I could to put a stop to it and, fortunately, I was successful. This does not make me a hero, however. I only did what any decent person would have. I would prefer no further media attention. Thank you."

And that was all the coverage I received. The local media moved on to the next tragedy du jour, forgetting all about me.

***

I returned home the Tuesday after the attack.

My forearm still ached and under the bandages was a nasty scar, but otherwise I felt mostly myself. The batting cages were out of the question for a while, though.

I had a supply of casseroles in the fridge provided by the ever-giving Juliette and the rest of the week on my hands. My plan was simple: rest, recover, and catch up on my reading. There's a lot to be said for downtime, especially after being so busy for so long.

Still, by Friday night I was getting bored. I ate the last of Juliette's casseroles and settled into the couch, pouring myself a glass of beer. My only plans for the evening were to have a few beers while I finished the classic science fiction novel I'd been reading.

I'd barely opened the book when there was a knock at the door.

Looking through the peephole, I practically jumped when I saw who it was.

"Ms. Davis-Wickham," I said, opening the door. "I mean, uh, Helena. Hello."

"Hello Trump," Helena said. "May I come in?"

"Of course. Come on in. I, uh, can I take your coat?"

"Certainly. Thank you."

Helena removed her coat. Underneath was a navy blue suit. The outfit looked expensive and fit her perfectly. My eyes glanced quickly at her figure as I took her coat.

"I hope I'm not disturbing you, Trump," she said.

"Not at all," I assured her. "Please, have a seat. Can I get you something?"

Helena noticed the full glass of beer on the coffee table.

"One of those would be great," she said.

"Right away."

I hurried into the kitchen and poured her a beer. Back in the living room, Helena was sitting on the couch with her legs crossed taking in the décor. I'd say my place was decorated better than most bachelors, but not by much.

"There you go," I said, handing Helena her drink.

I sat down on the couch next to Helena but careful not to sit too close. I took a sip of my beer as Helena did the same.

"I wanted to stop by and talk to you," she said. "I hope you don't mind."

"No, of course not."

Helena looked at my arm and its bandages.

"Does it still hurt?" she asked.

"Not so much anymore," I said.

"Good." Helena sipped her drink. "I'm glad."

"What about you?" I asked. "How're you holding up?"

"This whole thing is so overwhelming. Worst of all, every time I turn on the news it's all about fucking Wesley Reuben Jones. God dammit, why does it seem like the media always uses all three names with these guys?"

"I don't know," I said. "I think it goes back to John Wilkes Booth."

Helena nodded. She took another sip of beer.

"Trump, you saved me from a serial killer!" she blurted out, almost like she'd just realized it.

"The way I remember it, towards the end there, it was you who saved me from a serial killer."

Helena cast me a wry smirk.

"Did you know I'm a widow?" she asked.

"No, I didn't."

"My husband Craig, he died seven years ago. Massive heart attack at thirty-six. No warning signs whatsoever. He left me with a nine year old daughter. Erin's still not over losing him. My death would've crushed her."

Helena turned away, struggling to keep her composure.

I moved next to her, putting my arm around her shoulder. Regardless of my crush, it was an innocent gesture. Helena leaned close to me, resting her head on my shoulder.

I held her like that, neither of us saying a word. It was torture for me. The rational part of my brain wanted to comfort her in continued innocence, but feeling her so close and smelling her delicate fragrance drove the rest of me mad.

I resisted my impulses. Besides, I told myself, sex was probably the last thing on her mind.

Helena lifted her head and sat up. She shifted such that we faced one another. I stared into the depths of those endless green eyes and couldn't look away.

The next moment our lips were locked. I'm still not sure who initiated it. Maybe neither of us did, as sometimes these things have a momentum all their own.

I remember every tiny detail of that first kiss. It started out gentle and tentative, two pairs of lips seeking each other out carefully. That initial caution passed quickly, however, turning into eager exploration. I pushed my tongue against her lips and they opened.

Our tongues twirled around each other, my mind racing. I could scarcely wrap my mind around the incredible reality of the situation. I was kissing Helena Davis-Wickham. Not just kissing her, either. We were making-out, tongues dancing and hands groping each other.

"Trump," she murmured.

I kissed her neck and she moaned.

"I need you," she sighed. "Right now. Fuck me, Trump."

"Helena, are you sure?" I asked.

"I'm not some coy young girl, Trump," she said. "When I tell you I want you to fuck me, I'm sure."

***

We stumbled towards my bedroom, making-out on the way. Helena kicked off her high heels and we stood in front of my bed. I was out of my mind with lust by this point, pulling her close and kissing her on the mouth.

Reaching down, I undid the buttons on the front of her suit jacket. She let it slide off her shoulder and tossed it aside. Underneath was a white dress shirt buttoned down the front. It complimented her figure, especially her full bosom.

I kissed her neck, eliciting a happy gasp. I turned her gently around until I was behind her. I placed my hands on her hips and Helena swayed slowly underneath my touch, pushing her ass against my crotch.

I ran my hands up to her breasts and felt them through the fabric of her shirt. I leaned in and gave the back of her neck a gentle nibble. Helena responded, her breath quickening.

I moved my hands up and found the top button on her shirt. I undid it, leaning forward and kissing the side of her neck.

I undid the second button, still kissing her neck. Helena sighed quietly as I undid the third button, then the fourth. I slid my hands again over her breasts, feeling them now through her bra. They were as full as I'd imagined. C-cups if I had to guess, maybe even a D-cup.

A minute later I'd undone the remaining buttons, taking my time as I kissed her neck and we swayed sensuously against each other. I slid her shirt off and moved on to her skirt. One unbuttoning and unzipping later and it dropped to the floor.

Helena turned around and faced me in nothing but matching light blue bra and panties. She reached down and pulled my shirt up and over my head. She saw the bandages right above my hip where I'd been grazed.

"You poor thing," she said.

Helena touched the bandages gently.

"Helena will just have to do the work," she said. "We can't have you re-injuring yourself, can we?"

I pulled her close to me again, kissing her mouth. I reached down and undid her bra without too much fumbling. Her tits sprang free and I pulled her tight against me.

I reached down to feel her ass, appreciating its fullness as we kissed each other hard. Helena's arms roamed over my shoulders, arms, and back.

I slid my fingers under her panties and pushed them down. She shimmied out of them and, there she was, Helena Davis-Wickham naked in front of me.

As a younger woman, Helena could've been a swimsuit model. She still retained a stunning figure, though, enhanced by the advent of graceful maturity. My eyes ran over her big tits, soft contours, and lovely wide hips.

"Helena, this is a dream come true," I whispered.

Helena smirked, cocking her eyebrow playfully.

"Oh yeah?" she said. "Get ready for another dream to come true."

Helena sank to her knees and undid the button on my shorts. She unzipped them and pushed them down along with my underwear. My cock, partially-erect, popped free.

Helena looked it over.

"Very nice, Mr. Donald," she said in a mock-formal tone. "Most impressive indeed."

"Thank you, Ms. Davis-Wickham," I went along. "I thought you might appreciate it."

Helena took my cock in her hand. She grasped it by the base, stroking gently as she gazed up at me. She turned it upwards and licked the underside from right above my balls all the way to the tip. Then she licked up and down one side, then the other.

All the while her green eyes stared into mine.

Helena turned next to the tip, kissing it. I gasped as she flicked it lightly with her tongue. She kissed it again, her lips slowly parting and sliding over it. She pressed on, taking most of my seven inches into her mouth.

Helena had a talent for blowjobs. She held my cock at the base of the shaft, pumping me gently in precise rhythm to her sucking. All the while her eyes held my gaze as her head bobbed back and forth on my cock.

It was incredibly arousing, looking down and watching her suck my cock. I reminded myself of the crazy reality of it all. That was Helena Davis-Wickham down there, my unattainable crush, and she was sucking on my cock.

I thrust towards her mouth, unable to resist. Helena allowed me to thrust as hard as I wished, all the while controlling how much cock went into her mouth with her firm grasp around its base.

I began to groan loudly, lost in the ecstasy of it all.

"Oh fuck," I moaned. "Damn Helena, that feels good."

Helena sucked me for several more sweet minutes, finally easing off my cock and jerking me gently.

"You've a beautiful cock, Trump," she said.

"Thank you."

"Are you ready to fuck me with it?"

"Yes, ma'am."

"That's what I like to hear!"

Helena guided me onto the bed, gently positioning me on my back.

"You just lay back," she whispered, leaning over me and running her hands over my chest and shoulders. "Helena will take care of everything."

Helena crawled atop me, straddling my waist as she lowered herself onto my cock. She must have been aroused because I entered her without difficulty. Helena closed her eyes, sighing loudly, and began bouncing up and down on my cock.

It started out slowly but sped up after a few minutes. Helena reached down and rubbed her clit furiously, closing her eyes and groaning. Back and forth went her fingers in a rapid side-to-side motion. She was soon breathing rapidly, followed by a continuous low-pitched howl that exploded into a sustained shriek as she bucked wildly atop my cock.

I thrust upwards in time to her motion, reveling in the joy and wonder of the moment. Helena shrieked even louder but, when her orgasm began, she grew comparatively quiet. Her screams were replaced with a sudden, prolonged gasp as her fingers rubbed her clit rapidly and I thrust upwards.

A minute later I felt my own orgasm looming. When it arrived, its strength took me by surprise. I froze, delighting in the joy of release as my cock pulsed powerfully. On and on went the throbbing, until all that remained was the warm feeling of spent satisfaction that follows good sex.

Helena leaned forward, her body atop mine, and we kissed. I wrapped my arms around her and pulled her tight, her tits pressed against me. I realized I hadn't gotten a chance to suck and lick them. I resolved to correct the oversight someday as our tongues twirled and our lips danced in the happy calm of post-coital kissing.

***

Helena and I lay in bed afterward, holding each other tight. We were on our sides, looking into each other's eyes as I played gently with her boobs.

"Damn, Helena," was all I could think to say. "You're amazing."

"You're pretty nice yourself, kiddo," she said, kissing me gently. "I'm so thankful you were there when I needed you."

"Well I think you've thanked me pretty well!"

"Oh, Sweet Trump!" Helena laughed, caressing my arm. "Tonight wasn't about gratitude. After what happened, I needed an intimate connection. You went through the same attack, so who better to seek out?"

Helena paused, turning a thought around in her head.

"But you have a point." Helena kissed me again. "A young man such as yourself deserves to be thanked, thoroughly and properly thanked in a manner only a lady can do. Rest-up, Trump. Give it a week or two. Once you've recovered your full strength, Helena's gonna show you just how thankful she is."

CHAPTER TWO

It's strange, but I was happy to get back to work on Monday. After a life disruption like I'd been through, the return of routine was welcome.

I parked very close to where I'd been stabbed. Heading towards the elevator, I paused and looked over at the stairwell where it happened. I shuddered and walked on, wondering if I'd ever be able to go into work again without thinking about it. Probably not.

Of course, I reminded myself, some good had come of it all already.

I'd keep absolutely quiet about Helena and me. I didn't want to get her in hot water, for one, plus word getting out about us could hurt my own career. I could imagine getting a promotion someday only to have people question how I earned it. The fact that I'd nailed the hot boss lady was to remain absolutely secret.

It was a quarter to nine when I walked through the doors into our department. Doug had scheduled a meeting for promptly at nine.

Gina was at the front desk, staring at her computer screen.

"Hey," she said, not bothering to look up.

"Hey Gina," I responded, perplexed.

As I made my way towards the lab, a few coworkers saw me and said terse good mornings. I settled into my desk a bit peeved. I didn't expect a banner and confetti upon walking in the door, but everyone was acting as if nothing happened. Worse, in fact. They seemed almost hostile.

A pit formed in my stomach. Had they somehow found out about Helena and me? Did they think I took advantage of her? I was a worried mess by the time I entered the conference room and sat down. I scanned the faces there. Everyone seemed to be ignoring me.

Doug strode in, his usual grandiose self. He's a big guy in every way, tall with a protruding gut and a huge head.

"Good morning everyone," he said, launching right into his agenda. It turns out Helena had approved the plan we were working on the night I got stabbed. Doug explained it all in his loud, boisterous way of speech.

"Now comes the tough part," he was saying. "And that's implementation. At stake is nothing less than more efficient solar panels for a greener tomorrow, not to mention maintaining our industry leadership and increasing the value of your stock options. We have to work -"

Doug stopped mid-sentence, turning away. He started laughing.

"I'm sorry," he said. "I can't go on. I lasted as long as I could. Let's hear it for our man Trump, everyone!"

The room burst into applause. Everyone got to their feet clapping. I was at the center of a whirlwind of congratulations, guys slapping me on the shoulder and every girl in the department smooching me on the cheek.

Except for Gina, that is, who managed to plant a kiss on my lips in front of everyone without anyone so much as raising an eyebrow. She didn't normally attend staff meetings, but hung around the door to see my reaction to the big practical joke.

"It was Greg's idea," Doug explained. "He suggested we all act as if nothing had happened, just to screw with your head."

"Well, it worked!" I responded.

"Seriously, everyone," Doug continued. "This company was built on teamwork. Teamwork relies on good character, however, and Trump showed his character when one of the women of this company was being attacked. Now, Trump says he's not a hero. I'm not so sure about that."

We settled in for the meeting. Doug detailed all we'd be working on for the next year. I sighed, pondering the long hours ahead.

Gina approached me after the meeting broke up.

"Our Trump, the big hero!" she said. "What're you doing for lunch? Let me take you out, my treat."

"I've got a meeting with Human Resources over the stabbing," I said. It sounded like I was blowing her off but I corrected myself quickly. "How's Thursday?"

"Thursday's great!"

Gina walked off. I admired her curvy ass and thighs and recalled the feel of her soft lips pressed against my own, contemplating my situation. I'd just fucked the boss lady and now I'd made a date with the receptionist.

The complications arising from this could be myriad, but I didn't care.

***

I saw Helena that afternoon. I was returning from work following my lunch meeting with a Mrs. Turner from HR. She was nice, but I got the feeling she was mostly concerned with preventing me from suing the company. Hence the lunch HR was paying for. I told her as long as they agreed to pay the deductibles on my insurance and the days I missed were waived in terms of sick days, I'd sign whatever release she wanted.

"I think that can be arranged," she said, barely suppressing a relieved grin. They even threw in the standard workman's compensation for an injured arm. Not bad.

Helena was standing in the main lobby by the elevators when I returned from lunch. She was studying a file in her hands and talking to another corporate big wig. She wore a bright red suit and matching heels. Red was Helena's color, pairing well with her skin tone and pale blonde hair.

Helena glanced at me, a sly smirk forming in one corner of her mouth and an eyebrow cocking in my direction. She wore red-frame glasses, bringing out the iridescent green of her eyes even more than usual.

"Good afternoon, Mr. Donald," she said.

"Good afternoon, Ms. Davis-Wickham," I responded.

I grinned as I stepped into the elevator, replaying Friday night in my mind. I tried to recall every last sensation. I wanted to remember it all forever, from the taste of Helena's lips to the way her hair had the subtle aroma of vanilla. Most of all, I thought of the way her bountiful tits bounced steadily as she rode my cock.

We'd stayed in bed a long time after the sex was over the previous Friday, lounging together naked. I got up and got our beers. We drank them, snuggling and talking.

I lay in bed and watched her dress afterwards. It was like a reverse strip-tease, and surprisingly erotic. She slid her panties back on, then her bra. Reaching back, she hooked it without effort.

"How do women do that?" I asked. "You make it look so easy."

"It is easy, Sweet Trump," she teased.

I watched as she put her shirt back on and buttoned it up. She glanced at me, smiling. She enjoyed me watching her, and deliberately took her time.

On went the skirt, then the jacket, and finally her shoes. She studied herself in the mirror, nodding her head. A minute before, she was naked. Now she looked every bit the elegant and smart professional again.

I put on my shorts and shirt and followed her to the front door. We shared a long kiss as I wrapped my arms around her and held her close.

"I'll be in touch this week," she said. "We can talk more about getting you properly thanked."

"I'm looking forward to it," I said. "Come on, I'll walk you out."

Helena kissed me again after I walked her to her car. I went back inside and lay down in my bed. I could still smell her on the sheets and feel the warmth of where her body lay mere minutes before.

It wasn't long before I was hard again.

***

Gina greeted me Tuesday morning with a big smile. She was wearing a pink shirt which showed off her cleavage nicely. Her hair was back but a few raven tresses refused to cooperate and framed her face nicely.

"Hey, you!" she said.

"Hey, yourself!" I responded. I added, "You're looking nice, this morning."

"Thanks," she said.

A voicemail summoning me upstairs to Helena's office on my lunch break was waiting for me at my desk. Come lunchtime, I headed upstairs. I knew enough to be discrete, so I walked a few flights up the stairwell and then slipped into an upward-bound elevator unnoticed by anyone who knew me.

I'd never been to Helena's office before. It was way up on the tenth floor. Her secretary, a tall redhead, smiled as I walked in.

"Trump," she said. "Go right in."

Helena's office was like I might've imagined. It occupied a corner of our building with a magnificent view of downtown and contemporary art on the walls. She sat behind her glass-topped desk talking on the phone. She smiled, gesturing towards the chairs in front of her desk. I sat down.

"That's bullshit, Sam," she said sternly into the phone. "When? Why don't you call me when you know something more definite?"

Helena glanced at me. Her glasses were down around the tip of her nose and she looked like every naughty librarian fantasy I'd ever had, and I'd had plenty. She raised an eyebrow and smirked playfully.

"That's not acceptable," she said into the phone, her humorless tone in sharp contrast to the flirtatious look on her face. "Look, I'll give you to five and I think that's reasonable. See what you can do. Okay? Talk to you then. Bye."

"Hello, Sweet Trump," she said, putting down the phone.

Helena got up and came around the desk. She wore a navy blue suit and matching high heels, the skirt portion hugging her hips as she walked.

"How are you?" she asked, leaning over and giving me a quick peck on the lips.

"Good," I told her. "I keep thinking about Friday night."

"I'm sure." Helena sat down in the chair next to me. "That was the best fuck I've had in months. Time's short, so let me tell you why I asked you up here. My daughter's going to Washington this weekend on a JSA trip. They'll be leaving Friday afternoon and won't be back until Sunday evening. What I propose is simple."

Helena paused, a mischievous look in her eyes. She gave me her trademark smirk.

"I want to make myself available to you," she continued. "For the entire weekend. During that time, I will be at your complete sexual disposal. Do with me as you wish. Fuck me anyway you want. Let me thank you properly like I promised. How's that sound?"

"That sounds great," I managed to say.

"There's just one thing." Helena paused again. "Trump, an offer like this doesn't come along every day. Think about what you'd like, and don't be shy. I've been around the block. To give you an idea: If you want to fuck my ass, that's fine. If you want me to fuck your ass, for that matter, that's also okay. Don't squander this opportunity by being timid, Trump. Okay?"

"Okay."

"Go online tonight. Pick out some outfits for me and some sex toys, whatever you want. Print out whatever you want, bring it to me then, and I'll have it overnighted. Don't worry about price, either."

"I can do that," I told her.

"Great," she said, glancing at the clock on the wall. "Shit. I've got another appointment in five minutes. How's Thursday?"

"Um," I said. I didn't want to break my date with Gina. "Not good."

"How about tomorrow? Same time?"

"Sounds great."

"Tomorrow is better, after all, come to think of it," she said. "I'll be able to give you some time to talk some more. Bring your lunch."

We stepped towards the door. Helena kissed me hard again before I left then slapped my ass playfully.

I felt like I'd won the lottery.

***

I saw Helena the next day as we planned. I handed her the file I'd worked on. I'd spent hours online the night before, looking at outfits and lingerie I'd like to see her in. I finally settled on a few and printed them out.

Helena looked the pages over, nodding and smiling. Her glasses fell down to the tip of her nose again and it was my turn to smile. She wore a gray suit with a bright purple dress shirt and sat across from me at her desk with her legs crossed.

"Very nice," Helena said, looking over the first page.

"That's my favorite," I told her.

"I can see why." Her eyes flashed at me. "Red is my color."

"I know."

We wound up talking for a half hour. Helena quizzed me on my likes and dislikes, sexual and non-sexual. She nodded thoughtfully when I told her about my passion for Asian food. Then we switched to discussing my favorite sexual fantasies.

"I'll order everything tonight," she said when we were finished. "Trump, I'm so glad we had this talk. It's going to make everything so much more fun this weekend."

Helena handed me a paper with her address.

"I'm yours come six Friday," she said.

"Then I'll be there at six," I said.

I pulled her towards me and we shared a long, lustful kiss.

"Trump taking what he wants," Helena cooed. "Helena like."

"One more thing," I said.

"Yeah?"

"That first outfit I picked, you know, the red one?"

"Uh-huh."

"Be wearing it when I get there. And I'll be there right at six. I'm never late."

"Yes, sir," Helena growled. "And I'll have a special dinner waiting. You're gonna need your strength, kiddo."

***

Gina and I left for our lunch date right at noon the next day, hoping to get a table outside at a little Thai place a few doors down from our building. It was a gorgeous day, warm for late September.

Gina wore a green sweater buttoned-down in front over a yellow shirt and khaki pants, all chosen to show off her figure. It worked.

We got our coveted seat outside and ordered quickly from the lunch specials. A couple of guys from work caught sight of us and nodded enviously. Everyone loved Gina.

Gina glanced at the bandages on my arm.

"Does it still hurt?" she asked.

"No," I told her. "Not anymore. It hurt like hell for days, though."

"I can't imagine what was going through her mind when that guy grabbed her," she said.

"I'm sure she was scared," I said. "I was sure scared."

"She must be grateful to you."

I chuckled, then changed the subject as carefully as I could and asked Gina about herself. She was a fascinating girl, as it turned out. She played guitar, wrote songs, enjoyed cycling, and was a voracious reader. Still, my mind wandered back to Helena.

Gina walked close to me as we headed back to the office, our hands brushing casually a few times. I admired the way her hair behaved in the breeze and the way her big dark eyes were so expressive.

***

Friday was an agony of anticipation. I had a tough time concentrating, my mind wandering constantly to picturing the various positions I'd like to see Helena in and all the things I'd like to do to her. Would do to her, I corrected myself.

I had lunch again with Gina, this time in the cafeteria. She asked me what I had planned for the weekend. I told her a white lie.

"I'm visiting a friend," I said.

"Oh," she said. "That sounds nice."

Gina wasn't good at hiding her emotions. Disappointment flashed across her eyes, as clear as if the text of what she was thinking were displayed on them. She was hoping to see me that weekend and doing a bad job of disguising the face. She'd make a terrible poker player.

"We should do something after work one night," I said, shifting gears. "Maybe dinner next week?"

"Sure." Her eyes brightened. "Sounds great."

***

Helena lived in an upscale neighborhood from the 1920s in an old-money zip code, each home a unique architectural gem on spacious lots. Helena's home was a Tudor-style house surrounded by towering oak trees. It exuded good taste, and money.

I pulled into the long driveway one minute before six, true to my word. Grabbing my bag, I approached the door. I was about to knock when Helena opened it. She wore a long white robe closed in the front, but I could see the red gloves and boots which hinted at the outfit I'd picked out for her. She was wearing her glasses, too. By my specific request, she wasn't going to wear her contacts all weekend.

"Come on in, Trump," Helena said, a trace of a smirk crossing her face.

Inside her house was ultra-modern, in sharp contrast to the outside. Everything was sleek and spare, but with plenty of bright colors everywhere. Helena had lots of modernist furniture and vivid abstract paintings covered the walls. It looked like the kind of interior you see in an architectural magazine.

I closed the door behind me as I stepped inside. Helena cocked an eyebrow at me, undoing her robe and letting it fall to her feet the moment the door shut. She placed a hand on her hip in a provocative pose.

I stared dumbfounded, taking in the sight of Helena in the outfit I'd selected.

It started with her boots, high-heeled and reaching halfway up her thighs. They were bright red, complimenting her complexion perfectly. Next was the matching red corset with black laces up the sides. It fit tight, her ample boobs squeezed inside and threatening to pop out at any moment.

The matching gloves and corresponding collar around her neck provided the finishing touches, the little details which made the ensemble so great. Most of all, however, was the woman filling it out. Every inch of Helena radiated sex, from the spiked heels of her boots to the top of her blonde hair. I wanted nothing more than to take hold of her.

"Helena, Helena," I gasped. "You're a work of art."

"Glad you like it."

"Yeah, that's an understatement."

I stepped towards her and took her in my arms, grasping her tight. I kissed her hard and she wrapped her arms around my shoulders. We stood there making-out in her foyer, hands and tongues all over each other.

Somehow Helena detached herself. She was breathing heavily, her eyes afire.

"Plenty of time for that," she said. "Damn, this is going to be a fun weekend. Remember, I promised you dinner when you got here. Come on. Like I said, you'll need your strength."

Helena led me into the kitchen. It was large and modern with marble tops and a huge island in the middle. The large glass table was already set with a colorful feast.

"I thought I'd keep it light," she said, guiding me into a chair at the head of the table and sitting down on my right. "I remembered how you said you enjoyed Asian food."

"I'm obsessed with it," I said, taking in the magnificent spread laid out on the table.

Helena reached over and poured a bottle of beer into a tall glass and then poured herself the same.

"This is a Czech pilsner I think will go well with the meal," she explained.

I took a sip. It was smooth but with a strong element of hops.

"Excellent," I said. "I see you decided to cook Indian."

"You said it was a favorite."

"Indeed I did."

"Let me tell you what everything is," she said. "First we have curried shrimp with garlic and onions."

Helena pointed out a platter of bright yellow shrimp in an orange sauce arranged atop a glass platter. Bright green cilantro was sprinkled over the shrimp, creating a dazzling array of colors.

"Here we have the Paneer," Helena said, pointing out the dark green spinach dish.

"That's one of my particular favorites," I said.

"Finally, we have lemon-cumin rice," Helena added, gesturing towards a bowl of bright white rice with cumin seeds and cilantro sprinkled on top and sliced almonds and lemon zest mixed in.

"You cooked all this?" I asked.

Helena shrugged, a "who me?" look on her face.

"Helena Davis-Wickham," I said. "Renaissance woman."

"Don't praise me till you've tried everything," she cautioned.

Everything was cooked and flavored to perfection, no easy task with Indian food. There was a multi-layered spiciness to the shrimp, in particular, which made every morsel a flavorful delight.

We devoured everything on the table, draining our beers and chatting easily. Helena was nice to be around, not just beautiful but, I was learning, clever and funny.

Again and again my eyes wandered over her body as we dined. She noticed and turned it into a game, moving with deliberate, slow sensuality for me.

Taking a sip of beer, she cast me a smoldering look and held my attention. Taking up the glass with a gloved hand, she parted her lips as she brought it to her mouth. Still looking right into my eyes, she took a long sip and then lowered the glass. Her lips were wet from the beer and she licked them slowly with the tip of her tongue. Then she gave me a coy smile and looked like a school girl for a fleeting moment, feigning shyness.

The rest of dinner passed in that fashion, me staring at Helena and taking in her every move as she put on a slow, sensuous show. Every sip of beer and bite of food became sexual. When the meal was finished, we regarded each other silently. Neither of us had spoken for at least five minutes.

I placed my hand on her shoulder and she leaned towards me slowly. Her mouth parted, her tongue extending towards mine.

We kissed, our tongues pushing against each other. Helena let out a barely-audible sigh, our silence otherwise continuing unabated. I could taste the flavors of our meal on her lips and tongue, a subtle interplay of turmeric and cumin.

We stood, still kissing, our arms wrapped around each other. It was just like at the door before dinner, a frenzied lust taking hold of us. I nibbled Helena's neck, my hands wandering down to her ass.

Helena's eyes flashed, eyebrow cocking invitingly, and she took me by the hand. Silently, she led me upstairs to her bedroom. It was like the rest of the house, modern and clean. She had a queen-sized bed with a red comforter already pulled aside.

Helena turned around, posing for me again. She pushed me back to arm's length, a smoldering look in her eyes. She let her glasses dip down to the end of her nose and stared at me silently for a moment.

Stepping forward, Helena unbuttoned my shirt. She did so neither too rapidly nor too slowly. She pulled the bottom of my shirt out of my pants, pushing it off my shoulders. She reached down and pulled the underlying t-shirt up and over my head. I kicked off my shoes and slid off my socks.

Her face turned tender as she looked me over. My bandages were gone, but the scars remained. The cut on my side was barely anything, but the scar on my forearm was more noticeable. Helena gently touched my arm, her lip pouting in sympathy.

Reaching down, Helena undid my belt and unzipped my pants. She pushed them down along with my underwear and I stepped out of them. I was naked, erection already raging.

We kissed again, hard and long. We slid onto the bed together and lay side by side facing one another. Helena kissed my neck, sending quivers of pleasure expanding outwards from wherever her lips touched my skin.

Then Helena switched to my ear, flicking the earlobe with the tip of her tongue. She'd stumbled onto my most sensitive body part. I could be tired or stressed-out, and all a woman has to do is stick her tongue in my ear to get me going. No different this time. Helena read my reaction and struck, plunging her tongue into my ear. I moaned, the waves of pleasure she was creating almost too intense to take. When I couldn't take it anymore, I turned my head, seeking out her mouth, and we kissed.

I'd had enough foreplay and was ready to get down to business. I inched down her body, kissing every inch along the way. When I reached her pussy I lifted her legs and pulled her to the edge of the bed. I knelt on the floor, her pussy at the perfect height before me.

Few things in this life delight me more than eating pussy. I love everything about it: The aroma, the taste, and most of all using my tongue to make a woman come.

I leaned in close to her pussy. It was well-groomed, a pleasant patch of light hair on her pubic mound. I inhaled her aroma, a hint of musty goodness barely detectable. Helena must've showered when she got home from work, the light aroma the scent of her arousal.

I began with a long, slow lick, starting down at her perineum just above her asshole and moving up and over her clit. Helena gasped and I went right to her clit, licking it up and down eagerly.

Helena gasped and groaned, and on I licked. For long, happy minutes I licked her.

When I sensed Helena was duly warmed-up, I inserted my middle finger inside her vagina. Helena reacted with a happy moan and I angled the finger upwards to hit her g-spot, eliciting an audible chirp as I started fingering her steadily. I kept at it, licking her clit and fingering her pussy steadily.

I added a second finger, lapping up her juices with abandon. I licked her clit as fast and hard as I could manage, pausing only to breath now and then. All the while I fingered her with increasing speed.

Helena moaned loudly. It almost sounded like sobbing, it became so intense. I switched from licking her clit up and down to a sideways motion, recalling how she rubbed her clit while riding me the week before. Helena wailed uncontrollably.

"Oh!" she screamed. "Holy fucking shit! Oh, that's it!"

Helena grew suddenly silent, letting out a prolonged gasp as she came. I felt her pussy contracting on my fingers and I kept licking her pussy hard. Helena twisted violently, squealing loudly.

"Oh shit!" she gasped. "That's it!"

Helena's orgasm slowly subsided and I drew back. I climbed on top of her and kissed her mouth hard. I wanted her to taste her own juices. She didn't mind, kissing me back eagerly.

"Your turn, Sweet Trump," she whispered. "Go on, baby. Fuck the shit out of me."

I stood at the edge of the bed. Lifting Helena's legs, I moved my cock into position. She was soaked and stretched and I entered her in one easy thrust.

We were past gentle warm-ups by this point and I started out fucking her at a vigorous pace. She closed her eyes, moaning right away. I stared at her the whole time, admiring the curve of her torso in the corset.

After a few minutes, I gently maneuvered Helena so that she lay on her side. I still stood at the edge of the bed fucking her, only this time I lifted one leg up so that her thigh was tight against my stomach and her boot-clad calf pressed against my chest. I wrapped my arms around her leg, enjoying the feel. The additional traction it provided was a happy bonus.

Helena reacted at once to the new position, her eyes growing wide. She started to gasp right away, reaching down and rubbing her clit as I hammered her pussy.

I fucked Helena as rapidly as I could and she closed her eyes, her mouth contorting as she let out a long, low gasp. She fingered her clit back and forth and I knew she was having another orgasm.

My orgasm arrived a minute or two later, the remote tingle in my cock signaling its approach. I froze, the familiar mix of joy and release pulsing through me with each throb of my cock.

I pulled out of Helena and plopped down next to her.

***

"You've made me a sweaty mess," Helena said after a few minutes of quiet cuddling, sliding out of bed. "Vinyl doesn't breathe well, kiddo. I need another shower."

I watched Helena take off the outfit and started to get hard again as she stripped. She began by removing her gloves and then her collar. She unzipped her boots, took off her corset, and I sighed at the sight of her fully naked. To me, Helena would always embody the ideal combination of fit sexuality coupled with the mature mystique which pushed my buttons.

Helena put her glasses on her dresser and took a hair tie out from one of the drawers. I watched her put her hair up in a bun, admiring her round bottom. She went into the master bathroom and I heard water running a few moments later.

I shook my head in amazement. It hadn't even been ten minutes since my last orgasm, yet I was ready to go again just from watching Helena strip down.

I got out of bed and went into the bathroom. It had a huge shower with a glass door and two showerheads, all gleaming marble tiles and designer fixtures. Helena stood under the water, twin streams cascading over her chest.

Helena smiled at my entry, reaching over to slide open the door.

"I thought you might like to join me," she said as I stepped inside.

We kissed, the jets of hot water covering us. Already a light steam began to form as I took the soap from Helena's hand. It was one of those expensive artisanal soaps, light purple and scented with lilac.

I soaped Helena up, growing fully hard as I lathered up her arms, shoulders, and breasts. I gently moved her back under the water and rinsed her off.

My hands went up to her breasts. They were twin mounds of womanly wonder, slick and wet as the water poured over them. We kissed again.

I meant to wash her back. I meant to take my time and wash every inch of her. Honestly, I did.

"I've got to have you again," I told her instead. "Right now."

Helena looked at me, lust in her eyes. It had to be arousing for her to have a man half her age in her thrall.

"Then take me," she said.

Helena reached down and stroked my cock. I pressed her against the wall of the shower under one of the showerheads, the hot water flowing over my back as I kissed her neck.

"Fuck my pussy, baby," she moaned. "Right here, in the shower

"No," I whispered. "Not your pussy."

"Naughty boy." She smiled. "Helena like. There's lube in the top drawer of my end table."

I rushed out to the bedroom, nearly losing my footing in my haste. I found the lube right where she said it was and dashed back towards the shower.

Helena was bent over with her ass in the air, her arms propped atop a deep indented shelf built into the shower. I paused, admiring the soft curve of her butt and marveling at her confident, easy-going sexuality.

I squeezed plenty of lube onto my fingers and also onto her asshole. I smeared the lube over it, both streams of water cascading over my torso from either side.

I took my time, working in first one finger and then another.

"Oh, baby, that's so good." Helena encouraged me. "That's it."

I smeared some lube over my cock and moved into position, squirting Helena's asshole with still more. Slowly, I pushed the tip of my cock against her butthole. It yielded and I slid the head inside.

"Oh, fuck," Helena moaned. "Don't stop, baby. Keep going."

I paused, pulling back a slight bit. Then I pushed back in, this time a little further. Next I pulled out almost all the way, sliding in deeper yet again.

Soon I was fucking her ass nice and slow, enjoying the vice grip of her tight anus.

The fantasy of fucking a woman's ass in the shower had always been a favorite of mine, the subject of many shower jerk-off sessions over the years. I'd stand under the showerhead, furiously beating-off. Always, for some reason, it was anal sex I'd imagine. Not a blowjob, nor pounding a girl's pussy doggy-style. I'd just stand there and imagine I was fucking a woman's ass.

My pace picked up, Helena groaning steadily as the water blasted me from two directions. I closed my eyes, lost in the ecstasy and excitement of the moment.

Minutes passed. I've no idea how many. Ten or fifteen, perhaps. I was so turned on I would have come in no time if I hadn't just had an orgasm.

When my orgasm did arrive, it was even more powerful than the earlier one. The intensity of the experience and the fulfillment of my fantasy overwhelmed me. I froze mid-thrust, pushing myself into Helena's ass as far as I could. My cock throbbed, bursts of cum shooting up Helena's butt.

I pulled out of Helena and staggered back, knees weak.

The weekend was off to an excellent start.

CHAPTER THREE

Helena slipped-out of bed early but I didn't stir until nine. I lingered in bed, happily half-dozing and enjoying the indulgence of sleeping in. I finally crawled out of bed and stumbled to the bathroom, shaking off the last bits of happy slumber.

Two minutes later my teeth were brushed and my bladder empty. I headed downstairs, thoughts of the prior evening running through my mind.

The anal sex over, I bathed Helena like I'd originally intended. I soaped up every inch of her, from her cute little feet and long firm legs to her round, soft ass and her full breasts. I didn't forget her shoulders or her back, either.

Helena returned the favor, scrubbing every inch of me. We took our time and must have lingered under the water for a half hour, enjoying the feel of each other's bodies in a state of blissful satisfaction.

We toweled each other off and put on comfortable pajamas, the kind perfect for easygoing snuggling.

We split a bottle of wine and then another, lazing about the living room watching TV and talking for hours. I dimly recalled the draining of a third bottle. In the end we stumbled upstairs and fell asleep in each other's arms, drifting off into a deep drunken slumber.

I got to know Helena a lot more during our talk. I learned about her childhood and her family. Her father was a surgeon and she had an uncle who was a congressman for many years. Helena also starred at point guard from middle school through the Ivy League, putting her height and easy athleticism to good use. These days she was an avid runner and gym rat. She'd always been an avid reader, too, and it showed in her incredible breadth of knowledge. She could discuss virtually any topic with informed insight.

The conversation turned to sex. I wound up telling her everything about me in that regard, from my first fumbling attempts onward. Helena's own sexual past was far more fascinating, her college years of particular interest to me. She studied hard, fucked harder, and spoke about it all with an easygoing grace. She'd never been shy about sex, she explained, and always had a healthy libido.

Helena thought her sexual adventures over after marriage. A few years into juggling a career, studying for an MBA, and the arrival of an unexpected child, however, her marriage hit a wall. Helena wasn't specific, but hinted at a near-infidelity on her husband's part followed by a gradual transition towards an open arrangement.

"It was the only solution," she explained. "We were apart so much, and both of us oversexed. It solved a lot of issues."

Helena had lovers after her husband died, as well. I was the youngest, however, by more than a decade.

"I hope I measure up," I teased.

"And then some, kiddo."

***

I found Helena in the kitchen. She stood in front of the stove melting butter in a skillet. Assorted ingredients were on the counter next to her. She wore her pink pajamas from last night, her hair and make-up already done.

"Morning, babe," I said.

"Good morning, Sweet Trump!" she answered cheerfully. "Heard you stirring up there and thought I'd get breakfast going. Hope you've got an appetite."

"You know it."

I came up close behind her and slapped her ass gently. She twisted back toward me and we shared a long kiss and then she turned back to her cooking.

"Sit down," she ordered. "I've made coffee and poured you some juice."

"Thank you."

I watched Helena work as I sipped my coffee. She prepared everything in a calm, precise manner, her mind focused but also at ease. I could tell she knew what she was doing, and I wondered if she'd had professional training.

Breakfast was scrambled eggs with goat cheese, thinly-sliced chives sprinkled atop. They came served with a slice of rye toast on the side slathered with boysenberry jam. We ate at the big glass table in the kitchen.

I dug right in. The eggs were perfect, fluffy and delicate and balanced by the rich flavor of the goat cheese. The chives added both texture and another layer of flavor.

"I can't believe how well you cook," I observed.

"It's one of my two great passions in life," Helena said.

"What's the other?"

Helena cocked an eyebrow. I smiled.

"I know," she continued, sipping coffee. "Food and sex. I'm such a hedonist. The two are so similar, though."

"How's that?"

"Let's see," she said. "Both are multi-sensory, and sensual. Both, ideally, should be pleasurable. Both involve putting things inside one's body, as well as the bodies of others. Need I go on?"

"I think you convinced me."

"Never a doubt," she said. "So what did you have in mind for the day?"

"A few things," I said, finishing off my eggs.

"Such as?"

"Well," I replied, looking her over. "For starters, lose the pajamas."

Helena smirked, downing the rest of her coffee. She stood, pulling off her pajama top casually. She tossed it aside, her tits exposed in their full splendor. Next she shimmied out of her pajama bottoms and bright red panties.

"How's that?" she asked.

"So much better," I sighed. "Come closer."

Helena moved nearer. Reaching out, I ran my hands along the smooth firmness of her thighs. One hand went up over her hip, sliding along its curvature. My eyes fell upon her belly. In years past Helena might've had rock-hard abs. I preferred her forty-two year old waist, though, still trim but soft to the touch.

Helena's breasts were her crowning glory, though. They were large and full and topped off by large pink areolae. I looked up at her and Helena met my gaze. Her eyes were emerald-bright in the morning sunshine streaming through the picture window.

I took in the sight of her, my eyes wandering slowly over her curves. I love how gorgeous a woman in her forties can be. All the beauty of her younger years abides, now tempered and focused. Gone, as well, is the awkwardness of youth, replaced with a mature confidence and a grown-up sexuality.

Helena put her hand on my cheek, caressing it gently with the back of her fingers.

"Sweet Trump," she whispered.

Leaning over, I took one of her nipples into my mouth. Helena sighed, her hand moving to the back of my head as she took the other and placed it on my shoulder. I enjoyed her tits for a long time, sucking and caressing them.

My hand wandered over Helena's pubic mound. My fingers sought out her clit as her sucked a nipple hard and give it a little nibble. As I did so, I rubbed her clit gently and she let out a low moan.

I eased a finger into her pussy. I fingered her as I sucked and nibbled her breasts. Helena responded at once.

"Oh god Trump," she moaned.

Helena slid my shirt off my head. I pushed off my pajama pants and boxers. My cock was mostly erect. Helena reached down, stroking it to full hardness as she kissed me hard.

"What do you want me to do, baby?" she whispered. "I'm yours."

"Finger yourself for me," I said. "Right there on the island."

"Yes sir! You want a show, Sweet Trump, you're gonna get a fucking show."

Helena stepped back, her hips swaying and her eyes staring at me as she licked her lips slowly. I sat back, jerking off as I enjoyed the performance.

Helena bent over the edge of the island, arching her back and spreading open her ass cheeks. In the clear morning light I had an excellent view of both pussy and asshole, not to mention the beautiful round ass framing them.

Helena stood slowly, shaking her butt back and forth. She turned back to me and then hoisted herself onto the island. She lay back, sticking her legs straight up into the air. She reached both hands down to her crotch. With one hand, she inserted a finger and began to fuck herself with it. She used the other to rub her clit. She was soon fucking herself with two fingers as she rubbed her clit back and forth, moaning loudly.

I jerked off, but was careful not to come. I felt the distant approach of an orgasm and slowed-up. After the sensation faded, I resumed jerking off to Helena's performance.

Twice I backed-off from the brink of orgasm. All the while, Helena fingered and rubbed herself furiously. After a few minutes, she let out a low gasp as she reached orgasm.

I could've come right then and it would've been intense, but I wanted Helena on my cock first. I waited for her to catch her breath.

"Come here, Helena," I whispered. "Sit on my cock."

Helena smiled, sliding off the island and stepping towards me. She lowered herself onto my cock, easing me into her soaked pussy. She placed her hands on my shoulders and her feet on the floor to either side of me. Positioned thus, she used her strong thighs to move up and down on my cock.

Helena started slow but her pace soon increased, her big tits right above my face. I reached up and grabbed hold of them, squeezing gently as she continued bouncing up and down on my cock. Soon enough, I felt my orgasm impending yet again.

"Oh god Helena I'm gonna come," I moaned. "Please, I want to come on your tits."

"Go for it."

Helena slid off me and dropped to her knees in front of me. I stood, cock in hand as I jerked on it furiously. It was wet with Helena's juices.

My orgasm's arrival had retreated with the momentary pause in the action, but it soon returned with vigor. I pumped my cock hard and felt the surge of release looming. I gasped, lost in the happiness of relief as I felt that initial throb of delight. A burst of cum squirted forth and struck Helena's chest.

"That's it!" Helena exclaimed.

I jerked my cock again in time to the pulses, sending a second glob of cum splattering across her tits.

My cock throbbed on, the pulsations slowly subsiding in strength and intensity. I sighed, looking down at Helena.

Helena looked back up at me and smiled wickedly. Several globs of cum dribbled down her tits.

***

We cleaned up after breakfast, showering separately. I enjoyed sharing a shower with Helena but I knew she'd appreciate having her morning routine so I used the shower down the hall.

Helena took a half hour longer than me to get ready prepared for the day. I was downstairs reading when she joined me. She wore tight blue jeans and high-heeled brown leather boots along with a pale purple V-neck sweater I'm sure was cashmere. A simple gold necklace and matching emerald earrings completed her outfit.

Helena looked casual yet elegant, sophisticated yet sexy. The way her boobs stretched the fabric on her sweater was a certain head-turner, too.

"Helena Davis-Wickham in jeans," I teased. "Now I've seen everything."

Helena smirked, twirling around and sticking out her ass. The jeans hugged her butt perfectly.

"I could always change into something else," she joked.

"No need for that."

I was anxious to get out of the house for a while and spend some casual time with Helena. Fucking all day hour after hour until we collapsed exhausted wasn't realistic. Besides, part of the appeal of our weekend was me getting to simply be around her. There'd be plenty of time for sex later.

We drove over to a nearby park. It had a large lake and a walking trail meandering past ball fields and playgrounds. We held hands and strolled. The ball fields called to mind playing shortstop through college. I told Helena all about it. She smiled and grasped my hand tighter.

We caught a few looks, which I expected. A pair of guys my age walking by nodded grinning, no doubt wishing they were in my place. A few minutes later a pretty lady Helena's age glared at us. Who knows what goes through people's minds?

Helena insisted she take me to one of her favorite cafés for lunch. It was in the business district on a side street dotted with art galleries. It was unassuming in appearance and we sat outside in the adjacent cobblestone courtyard. The chairs and tables were all bright orange and there was a tree growing in the center providing some shade.

Our waiter approached and greeted Helena by name. He was a tall guy my age.

"Do you trust me to order for us?" Helena asked me.

"Implicitly."

Helena barely glanced at the menu. She ordered us a pair of India Pale Ales and began pointing to various menu items.

"We'll start with the duck fat fries," she said. "For the charcuterie course, we'll go with the -- hmm, let's see -- let's do the coppa picante and the lardo. For cheeses I think the cambozola and the manchego. For my entrée, I feel like the halibut."

"Excellent." The waiter nodded, scribbling our order. "And for your friend, Helena?"

"He's not my friend, Todd." Helena managed to sound both serious and playful, never looking up from the menu. "He's my lover."

"Then he's a lucky man," Todd replied, with hardly a pause. "What would he like in terms of lunch?"

"Do you like scallops, Trump?" Helena asked.

"I love them."

"He'll have the scallops."

Todd took our menus, casting me a jealous grin before leaving.

"I take it you've been here a few times?" I said.

"I'd say twice a week since it opened last year," she said. "Poor Todd. He's been panting after me the whole time. I should put him out of his misery and just fuck him already."

Lunch was among the best I've ever had. Todd brought us our beers and the duck fat fries came out a few minutes later, served in a mason jar with garlic aioli. We ate the fries and talked, watching people walk by on the street.

Next came the charcuterie plate, an assortment of cheeses and cured meats served on a wooden board with a baguette and a dollop of the spicy house mustard. It was all fantastic, as were our entrees.

We were just stepping out onto the street afterward, hands grasped, when we ran into two of Helena's friends walking in.

Helena introduced them. Their names were Kate and Hannah. Kate was tall and thin with long blonde hair, beautiful blue eyes, and a broad smile. Hannah was a short, curvy brunette with glasses and light hazel eyes. They were both hot ladies in their forties like Helena and had an unmistakable air of urbanity.

Hannah, in particular, caught my eye. Her pretty eyes under dark eyebrows, full lips, and ample bosom all stood out to me. There was also a mischievous look in her eyes and a touch of lustiness in her smile I picked up on at once. She glanced at me, her eyebrows raised subtly, then back at Helena.

Helena introduced me.

"Trump!" Hannah and Kate exclaimed in unison.

The next thing I knew these two elegant ladies were hugging me and giggling like school girls. I received kisses on the cheeks from both.

"Our hero," Kate said.

"I, um," I stammered. "I only did what seemed right."

"We're glad you did," Hannah said. "You saved our Helena. Well! You two enjoy the rest of your day. Call me, Helena."

Hannah glanced at Helena again, Helena cocking an eyebrow at her. Some kind of nonverbal message was conveyed between them. Whatever it was, I had no idea.

"I hope I didn't embarrass you," I said after her friends had gone inside.

"Are you kidding?" Helena laughed. "They're seething with jealousy right now."

Helena kissed me on the mouth and I wrapped my arms around her. We kissed right on the street and walked off holding hands.

***

We grabbed some espresso after lunch at a little coffee bar around the corner from the restaurant. It had bare brick walls covered with funky art work for sale. We sat and talked for a long time.

There was a simple joy in the act of sitting and talking with Helena. Although I was starting to feel horny again I was in no rush to get back to her house. In the afternoon light, the emerald brilliance of her ever-changing eyes deepened into a darker shade of green altogether. My mind wandered contemplating their depths.

Conversation turned towards me and my life. Helena listened to me talk about college and how I was close to Juliette and a small group of friends I'd known most of my life.

"Any young women in the picture?" she asked.

"I, um," I faltered.

"You're going to act shy now?" she whispered playfully. "Remember me? You know, the lady whose ass you fucked last night? The one whose tits you came all over after breakfast?"

"Yeah there's one," I said.

"That cute little receptionist?"

I stared at her in astonishment.

"I saw you two having lunch the other day. I wasn't stalking you, just rushing to a lunch meeting down the street. Good for you, by the way. She's gorgeous."

"I don't know how interested I am in her," I said. "I mean, after being with a woman like you, it's hard for a girl her age to measure up."

Helena cocked a skeptical eyebrow.

"No, I'm serious. Girls my age, they're just so damned dramatic and coy and silly. I prefer someone more mature, not just in body but in mind."

"You should give her a chance, Trump. She might surprise you. Not trying is the only way to ensure your chances of success remain zero."

***

We'd scarcely stepped inside Helena's house when I turned towards her. I wrapped my arms around her shoulders and we shared a long, luscious kiss.

"Someone's ready for more Helena," she murmured.

"You have no idea how ready. You've been driving me nuts all day."

"How do you want me?"

"Later I want to do it to you raunchy, really raw and nasty," I said.

"Oh! Helena likes the sound of that."

"But I want something else first."

I explained and Helena listened. When I was done she kissed me tenderly.

"Give me five minutes head-start," she said.

With that she turned and went upstairs. I waited, checking my watch every thirty seconds, and went upstairs when it was time.

I'd had sex with Helena four times, but this time was going to be different from the rest. This time, I wanted us to have sex that was tender and loving. There'd be time for crazy fucking later, but I knew I'd always regret it if I never made love to Helena.

Helena had everything ready. The lights in her bedroom were turned down low, just dim enough to add some mood but not so dark as to impair one's view. A piano concerto played on the radio on her nightstand and Helena lay on her side waiting for me. She wore a simple white silk nightgown with thin shoulder straps and a V-neck showing off her cleavage.

My eyes journeyed over her, admiring her full breasts, the curve of her hip under the white silk, and her long legs.

I smiled and said nothing, sliding off my shirt and wriggling out of my jeans. I took my socks off but left my underwear on and crawled in bed with her. Our faces inched closer until our mouths were mere inches apart.

"Are you ready for me, Sweet Trump?" she whispered.

We kissed. Helena acted timid at first, as though trying to recreate a first kiss with someone new. Her lips parted ever-so-slightly, however, and things grew steadily more passionate. Soon, our tongues and lips were attacking each other with growing enthusiasm.

It lasted a long time, a symphony of tongues and lips twirling and licking in perfect harmony. Helena's hands explored my arms and shoulders, running down my back. She murmured and cooed, enjoying my smooth muscles. My hands caressed her face then traveled down her back, as well. They journeyed over the soft curve of her hip and across the smooth expanse of her legs.

Helena's hands found my penis, reaching inside my underwear. Despite all the orgasms of the last twenty-four hours, I was soon fully erect. She pushed my underwear down and off.

I lay there naked, the feel of the smooth silk of her nightgown against my skin. Slowly, she pushed me onto my back and crawled atop me.

We kissed wildly all the while, our tongues warring as Helena's weight pressed down against me.

Helena took my penis in hand and guided it towards her pussy. The tip pushed against her vaginal opening and I could feel her moistness. She must have been intensely aroused, my cock sliding in smoothly a moment later.

Helena started kissing my neck, her tongue flicking my earlobe a few times and sending me through the roof. I was aloft in pleasure, my hands on her ass as she rocked back and forth on my cock.

Helena sat up, slipping her nightgown up and over her head. I placed my hands on her hips, enjoying their feel as I watched her breasts bounce slowly up and down as she rode me.

"Oh my god that feels so good," she moaned, moving faster.

"Yeah? You like my cock in you?"

"Oh yes."

I reached up, massaging her breasts. Helena groaned and closed her eyes, face pointing upward. She reached down and began rubbing her clit, bucking wildly a few minutes later as she enjoyed her orgasm.

Catching her breath, Helena smiled broadly and leaned in over me. I wrapped my arms around her and pulled her close, savoring the feeling of her fully on top of me as we kissed.

I rolled us over without pulling out of her. We kissed, Helena's hands grabbing my ass cheeks as she let out a gentle sigh. I started drilling her hard, desire carrying me along. We kissed wildly, moaning the entire time.

Helena wrapped her arms and legs around me and I fucked her with ever-increasing zeal. We were tangled around each other, our mouths locked in a fury of passion as I fucked her.

It was one of the best orgasms of my life. I felt it coming long in advance, hammering her pussy in eager anticipation of release. When my cock started throbbing, it was with a force and intensity I'd scarcely ever experienced. As the waves of pleasure splashed over me, I could only gasp.

I rolled off Helena and lay there, catching my breath. The last few minutes, I'd been pounding her so furiously it wound up a workout. Helena rolled over, resting her head on my shoulder as I put an arm around her. I kissed the top of her head as she caressed my chest.

"Goddamn," I said. "That was..."

"Pretty good, huh?"

"Yeah."

We cuddled for a long time, talking quietly.

"Any thoughts for dinner?" Helena asked. "There's a Vietnamese place around the block."

"I could go for some pho."

"We could order take-out," she suggested. "That way we can lounge around here and never actually get fully-dressed again today. What do you say?"

"I say it sounds good."

"Excellent. I'm tired. Fancy a nap?"

"Also sounds good."

"Okay, no more talk. Only one last thing."

"What's that?"

"Fuck me however you want tonight, but leave tomorrow to me."

"Did you have something in mind?"

"You could say that."

"What?"

"It's a surprise."

"A surprise? What -"

"Hush, you." Helena placed a finger to my lips. "Not another word. All you need to know is I've something very special in mind for you tomorrow. Now rest."

"Okay," I mumbled, mid-afternoon drowsiness combined with sex starting to take its toll.

Five minutes later I was fast asleep.

CHAPTER FOUR

I spread Helena's ass cheeks apart and moved into position. She was naked save for a pair of black fishnet stockings and matching high heels. She was on all-fours, her hands tied to her headboard.

The TV on the wall played a favorite porn scene I'd selected. It featured a hot actress in her forties. The MILF was a blonde like Helena, with nice tits and a gorgeous ass. She was on her knees going back and forth sucking on a trio of large, hard cocks.

That afternoon, the sex between Helena and I was warm and romantic. It was going to be much different this time, however. I was in the mood for raw and raunchy, feeling like pushing the envelope. Helena and I went over some of my ideas and she was game for them.

Whatever Helena had in mind for my big surprise tomorrow, she wouldn't say. I decided not to dwell on it and focus on the fun we were about to have.

"You like what you see up there on the TV?" I demanded, feigning an angry, interrogatory tone and doing a poor job of it.

"I do," Helena whimpered, pretending shame.

I tried to suppress a grin but failed. I'd never even attempted any kind of role play or light bondage like this. I knew I'd no idea what I was doing but didn't care. It was only going to be fun if I didn't take myself too seriously.

"You'd like that to be you, wouldn't you?" I asked.

"Yes, sir. I'm a dirty girl. I can't help it I love cock so much."

"You'd like to suck those cocks, wouldn't you?" I slapped her ass, not too hard. "Answer me."

"Yes."

"Then you'd like to fuck them, wouldn't you?"

"Yes."

"You'd make them all come, wouldn't you?"

"Yes."

"You want cock right now, don't you?"

"Yes, sir."

"Well, you're going to have to wait."

"Please! I need it now."

"Too bad."

I reached over and picked up the butt plug. It was a glass model, several inches thick. I smeared lube over it and put a dab on my finger, rubbing it on her asshole.

"Oh, that's it," Helena moaned, holding up her end of the game. "I love it when my asshole is teased."

"What else do you like guys doing to your asshole?"

"I like when they finger it."

"What else?"

"I like when they fuck it. Long and hard."

"Is that all?"

"I like when they lick it."

I started in surprise, for some reason not expecting that last answer. Something about the idea took hold of my imagination, though. The thought of licking an asshole wasn't something I'd ever given much thought to before that moment.

I put the butt plug back down and spread her ass cheeks apart. There was her lovely little butthole. I contemplated my sudden, unexpected urge. I knew she'd prepared herself thoroughly for anal play, douching and scrubbing down there thoroughly after dinner.

On the screen, the MILF was riding a cock, bouncing up and down as she jerked and sucked-off the other two erections. I looked back at Helena's ass.

"You like your asshole licked, do you?" I demanded.

"Oh, yes sir."

"You want me to lick it?"

"Please."

"Please what?"

"Please lick my ass, sir."

"What? What'd you say?"

"Please lick my ass, sir!"

Almost without thinking, I found myself plunging my face into her ass. It may have violated the whole domination game we were playing, but I made up my mind to follow things wherever they led.

I flicked her asshole with my tongue and a shudder passed through her body.

"Oh, fuck," she moaned.

I licked her asshole again, this time applying firmer pressure.

"Is that what you like?" I asked.

"Yes, sir! Oh, fuck yes!"

I gave Helena a few more firm licks and she started squealing. Before long she was bucking and moaning wildly. On I licked, loving her uncontrolled howling. She was breathing rapidly, writhing and squealing.

"Holy fucking shit, I can't take it anymore!" Helena screamed. "Please, just fuck me! This is too much!"

I withdrew, slipping a still-lubed finger in her ass. I fingered her butt and her breathing calmed, her howling easing into a controlled moan. I slipped a second finger into her ass, spreading her sphincter.

"Oh god I'm so fucking horny!" Helena howled.

I picked up the butt plug with my free hand. Withdrawing my fingers, I slipped it in, pushing it through Helena's asshole. She cried out, her sphincter stretched more than she enjoyed for a moment.

"Oh, that's better," Helena moaned as the plug settled into place. "Now my ass feels nice and full."

Rising, I positioned myself behind Helena. I reached down and sought out her vagina. Her pussy was drenched, wetter than I'd ever known her to be. I eased my cock into place and then buried it inside her. I could feel the butt plug's presence pushing against my cock from above, an unusual sensation but not unpleasant.

I looked up at the screen as I began to slowly fuck Helena. The MILF was on all-fours, a cock ramming her from behind while she alternated sucking off the other two.

"Fuck me good, Trump," Helena moaned. "Fuck me good. That's it, nice and hard."

I sped up my pace, slapping Helena's ass. She started moaning and talking to me, a grand performance for my benefit.

"That's it, that's it," she squealed. "Oh fuck I feel so full! Oh my God I love it like this!"

On the screen, the MILF was straddling one of her gentlemen friends, leaning forward and rocking back and forth on his cock. She sucked a cock thrust in her face. As I watched, the third man moved into position behind her and entered her ass.

The three actors began drilling her simultaneously. I stared at it wide-eyed as I fucked Helena, hammering her pussy with vigor.

Helena played her role perfectly.

"Oh, that's it," she sighed. "I feel like I've got two cocks in me back there. Keep fucking me, baby. Fuck me!"

Helena moaned incoherently, growing ever louder until her shrieks echoed against the walls of the bedroom. I reached forward and grabbed her hair with both hands, pulling back on it. I was careful not to hurt her.

"Fuck yeah!" she howled, her face yanked upwards. "That's it! Pull my hair! Harder!"

I obliged her, yanking her hair with both hands. I was still tentative, though, afraid of causing real pain.

"Harder!" she shouted. "Harder! I said pull it harder, motherfucker! So I can feel it!"

I gave her hair a good yank and Helena shrieked loudly, her back arching sharply. The whole time, I was drilling her as fast as I could.

"That's it!" she screamed. "That's it! I'm gonna fucking come!"

Helena let out a prolonged, incoherent squeal followed by a loud gasp. I fucked her with all my might as she came shuddering and gasping.

I soon felt the first, remote indications of my own orgasm. By then the MILF on screen was on her knees with her mouth wide open, her gentlemen suitors jerking off over her face. The first actor came, his money shot landing on her tongue.

"Let me taste your cum, Trump," Helena moaned. "Don't you want to come in my mouth, baby? Just like her."

I pulled out and scrambled in front of her, sitting on the headboard and facing her mouth. Her hands were tied below me and my cock pointed right at her mouth.

I started jerking off, my cock still wet with Helena's juices. Her mouth was scant inches from its tip.

"Oh my," she cooed. "What a view."

I couldn't help but grin. She was so game for anything, it was intoxicating. Her eyes flashed and she smiled, looking up at me.

"That's it, baby," she encouraged me. "Jerk off for Helena, squirt that sweet cum in my mouth."

On the screen, the second actor was jerking off. His cock loomed over the actress's face, squirts of cum striking her cheek and chin.

"I'm gonna cum," I gasped.

Helena leaned forward and took the head of my cock into her mouth. She held it there and applied gentle pressure with her lips as I finished jerking off. My cock was soon throbbing, each pulse sending another burst of cum into her mouth. Helena held her mouth in place the entire time.

Thirty seconds after the initial burst of orgasm, the last tiny pulsations faded into memory.

***

I threw on my shorts and a t-shirt, heading downstairs while Helena showered. My phone was on the island in the kitchen. I picked it up and checked it, a dozen messages awaiting me. I frowned. I'm an oddball for my generation in my attitude towards my phone. I see it as a tool, and a useful one at that, but more often than not I consider it a nuisance.

I scrolled through the texts, all telling me the same thing.

"Holy shit," I said.

Nearby Helena's phone was chirping, her own messages streaming in. I texted Juliette back first and then worked my way through responding to the others.

Helena came down wearing one of my t-shirts and nothing else. I couldn't help but note how amazing she looked.

"You'd better check your phone," I told her.

"What is it?"

"Wesley Reuben Jones is dead."

"Holy shit! How?"

"They don't know yet," I told her.

Helena picked up her phone. She had a backlog of messages, all from friends and family who'd heard about Jones's death. She went into the living room and turned on the TV, switched to the local news channel, and sat on the couch. I joined her and we waited for something on Jones.

A few minutes later the report on his death came up.

"A shocking development tonight in the case of accused serial killer-rapist Wesley Rueben Jones," the anchor said. "Diane Genovese is standing by with details."

"That's the reporter who wanted to interview me," I said.

Diane came on the screen. She was standing in front of the county jail, microphone in hand.

"Questions abound this evening in the death of accused killer rapist Wesley Reuben Jones," Diane said. "Multiple sources have confirmed that Jones is dead and an investigation into his death is ongoing. Jones, you may recall..."

Diane went on to recount the whole case. In reality, nothing was said beyond Jones was dead and the cops hadn't yet said what happened.

"I don't feel sorry for the bastard." Helena said calmly when the story ended. "But I was looking forward to his getting sentenced and us sitting there in court for it."

Helena's phone chirped again. She glanced at it.

"It's my daughter," she said.

Helena took the call in the other room. After the Jones story, a piece about a broken water main began. I turned the TV off.

"Her friend texted her with the news," Helena said when she returned.

"What'd she say about it?"

"She's okay with it, actually." Helena turned her phone off and tossed it on the coffee table. "I need a drink, a real one. How about you?"

***

I woke up the next morning, rolling over and staring up at the ceiling. I felt surprisingly well considering Helena and I split most of a bottle of high-end bourbon the night before. My mouth felt dry and there was a mild, dull ache behind my eyes.

Helena was nowhere to be found. A note next to the coffee maker said she'd gone to the gym early and would be back with bagels.

Shrugging, I poured myself a cup of coffee. I checked my phone for more news about Jones. The news was saying he'd killed himself. Shrugging, I closed the window and looked over the college football scores from the day before. The dose of caffeine banished my headache after a few minutes.

Helena came home, a bag from the bagel store in one hand and the Sunday newspaper in the other. She wore tight black workout pants, sneakers, and a powder blue fleece jacket.

Helena dropped the bagels and the paper on the island and took off her jacket. Underneath was a purple t-shirt that clung to her nicely.

"Good morning, Sweet Trump," she said pleasantly.

We kissed.

"Hungry?" she asked.

"Sure," I said. "Did you hear about Jones? Suicide."

"Saw it on the news at the gym. Couldn't happen to a nicer person."

We spent a good portion of the morning on the couch together eating bagels, sipping coffee, and working through the Sunday crossword together. It was fun leaning close together as we puzzled over the clues. We joked, teased, and debated possible answers.

I know people who can solve the Sunday crossword in no time. Helena and I aren't them. Even with Helena's MBA and my engineering degree, it took us over an hour. We got it done, though, sharing a celebratory kiss when the last clue was filled in.

"I enjoyed that," I told her.

"I'm glad. Me too."

"Was that my big surprise?" I teased.

"Not by a long shot." Helena glanced at the clock. It was nearly eleven. "Shit. I've got to get ready. I suggest you clean up, too."

***

Whatever it was Helena had in mind for me, I could only guess. My imagination roamed through possible scenarios as I showered and shaved. Even through a light lunch of grilled veggie sandwiches, my mind wandered. Helena seemed distracted, too, checking her phone whenever it chirped. The last time, she grinned and put it aside and we finished lunch.

"You ready?" Helena asked me.

"I hope so."

"Here's what I want you to do. Go upstairs and go into the guest bedroom, the one facing the backyard. Strip down, all the way. You'll find a blindfold on the bed. Put it on, lay down, and wait. I'll try not to be too long."

Two minutes later I found myself naked on the bed upstairs, a black leather blindfold over my eyes. The queen-sized bed had the comforter already pulled-back when I went upstairs, the blindfold on the pillow waiting for me.

Ten minutes must've passed before I heard Helena enter.

"Hello, Trump," she said, a hint of mischief in her voice.

"Hello," I answered.

"Your cock's not hard," she observed with mock distress. "Make it hard, Trump. Go on."

I reached down and stroked my cock, the knowledge Helena was there watching helped build my arousal. Before long, I had a respectable erection.

"That's much better," Helena announced. "Now, Mr. Donald, are you ready for the best fuck of your life?"

"Bring it on."

I felt the bed depress as Helena slid into next to me on my right. Her hand touched my arm. I was awash with anticipation, still wondering what she'd planned.

Then I felt the weight of someone climbing onto the mattress on my left.

"What?" I said, startled.

"It's okay, Trump," said a woman's voice on my left. It had the timbre of someone Helena's age.

"I hope you don't mind," Helena whispered. "I invited a friend."

I relaxed, overjoyed as gentle hands caressed my shoulders and chest from both sides of me. The thought of this scenario had occurred to me, of course, but I dared not expect it. It was the final culmination of a growing realization about Helena. I'd come to understand that she was a rarity, far more sexually uninhibited than the large majority of women. Again and again, she'd been game to whatever crossed my mind. And now this.

"Who are you?" I asked.

"Call me Marie," the newcomer said.

"Marie," I repeated. "That's a pretty name."

I could feel Marie as she leaned close against me. She was naked, her smooth warmth rubbing against the length of the left side of my body. She placed one hand on my chest, her other hand stroking my hair.

Helena did the same, pushing close against me as her hands explored my body. Neither woman touched anywhere near my cock, though.

Marie kissed me first. It took me by surprise, blindfolded as I was. First there was the feel of long hair against my cheek and neck as she leaned in. Then I felt the warmth of her breath. A moment later was the sudden press of moist lips against my mouth.

My lips parted, ready for our tongues to perform their lovely duet. Instead Marie used her tongue to lick my lips, slowly sliding her tongue over them. She started with my upper lip and then moved across my lower lip before repeating the process in the opposite direction.

I'd never experienced that particular move before and found it incredibly hot.

Marie plunged her mouth against mine, our tongues dancing. Her lips were softer and fuller than Helena's and she also had a different style of kissing. Where Helena's kisses were aggressive and wanton, Marie's were softer and wetter. I'd never be able to decide which I prefer. Each had its particular merits.

Helena began kissing my neck. The feel of two sets of lips and the bare skin of two women pressing against me sent me into overdrive. I felt a hand on my penis at last. It took me a moment to realize it was Marie's. A second hand, this one Helena's, reached down and gently caressed my balls with her fingertips.

I found my head being gently turned back towards Helena's mouth, Marie switching to my neck. I could've lain there forever, my mouth switching back and forth between Helena and Marie. It was an experience more joyous than I'd dared to expect. If there's a Heaven, I got a glimpse of what it must be like.

Then they took it to the next level.

They moved off my mouth and started kissing the sides of my neck. They were both stroking my cock by this point, Helena grasping the base with her gentle touch as Marie's fingers slid back and forth over the tip.

They eased their mouths upward, sticking their tongues in my ears simultaneously. The burst of pure, raw pleasure was so intense I could scarcely stand it. I let out an incoherent moan, my chest heaving as I writhed in ecstasy.

I've never tried hard drugs but I can't imagine the most powerful narcotic could produce anything better. I had not one woman but two working my most sensitive body part and it was sending me into the stratosphere. I'm sure it was by design, too, as Helena knew all about my sensitive ears.

"Oh my god," I moaned over and over. "I can't take anymore."

They showed me no mercy, only removing their wiggly wet tongues periodically to nibble my earlobes. It was like changing the chord of a melody, altering the specific nature of the pleasure but retaining its basic intensity.

I broke off, unable to take it any further. I turned my head towards Helena, kissing her furiously as Marie leaned in and kissed the back of my neck. I let out a growl. Turning back to Marie, I kissed her mouth hard.

"Someone's aroused," Helena whispered.

"Damn straight," I said. "I'm so ready for both of you."

Helena slid down my torso, kissing my chest and stomach as she went along. I kissed Marie, my hands seeking out her tits.

Helena took my cock into her mouth, swallowing the head and sucking hard.

I made-out with Marie with abandon. Our tongues attacked each other and I pawed her tits desperately. My hands explored Marie's body, getting a sense of her. She was curvier than Helena, and probably shorter.

Helena's head bobbed up and down in a steady rhythm on my cock and I pulled Marie closer. Marie leaned over me, her tits pressing against my face. I sucked on the nearest of her nipples eagerly.

Helena sensed I'd come right away if she kept going. She slowed her pace to a languid one, her mouth easing up and down my entire length as if in slow motion.

"I have to get a piece of that," Marie said and started to slide down my torso.

"Swing your legs up here," I told her.

Silently, Marie pivoted until she was on all fours with her head facing my cock and her ass next to my chest. I reached out and explored the contours of her rear end with both hands. Her ass was bigger than Helena's, its feminine roundness accentuated by being stuck in the air. Marie was definitely a plump little MILF.

She was also a good cocksucker, as it turned out.

Helena lifted her head off my cock, keeping hold of the base. She pointed it towards Marie and the women shared a giggle. I wondered if this was the first time they'd shared a cock. Given the ease with which they interacted in bed, I doubted it.

Marie took my cock in her mouth and sucked it vigorously. It felt different than Helena's mouth, coming in at a different angle. It was like how a woman sucking your cock in the sixty-nine position produces a distinct sensation from a regular blowjob.

They took turns sucking on me, each working its magic before switching off. Sometimes they would get fancy, both ladies running their tongues up the sides of my cock or Helena licking my balls as Marie sucked.

You'd think I'd have come right away. The pauses when the ladies switched off blunted any looming orgasm, however. I could've lasted an hour before coming.

I reached down and gently pulled Marie's ass closer. She read my cues and swung her right leg over my shoulder and lowered her ass onto my face as she settled her torso onto mine. I could feel her tits pushing against my stomach as she leaned over and sucked my cock, Helena gently flicking my balls with her tongue.

I lifted my head, my hands on Marie's plentiful butt cheeks. Burying my face in her pussy, I gave her a long lick to start things off. To my great delight, I discovered Marie's pussy was nice and musty, her wonderful strong aroma filling my nostrils.

Marie sighed as I licked her pussy furiously. I found her clit and worked it with my tongue, licking first up and down and then switching to side to side. For variety I gave her clit gentle little sucks which made her gasp and moan.

I licked her pussy for some time, inserting a finger into her dripping vagina. I fingered her rapidly, still licking as hard as I could manage. It became harder for her to focus on sucking my cock and Helena took over most of that task. I inserted a second finger, pumping rapidly and licking happily.

Helena backed off sucking my cock, not wanting me to come yet. She stroked it gently and whispered at Marie.

"That's it, sweetie," she told her. "That's it, come for us. Come for us."

"Oh, I'm so close," she moaned. "Keep at it, Trump."

A minute later Marie's entire body shuddered and her pussy constricted three or times on my fingers. I fingered her as fast as I could even though my arm was starting to hurt.

I pulled out my fingers out and Marie rolled off me. Her body was half-draped on my left side, one leg resting against my shoulder and her face by my hip. One of her arms lay atop my stomach, her hand atop my quad.

"Oh fuck," Marie said, catching her breath. "You were right. He's good with that tongue."

"What'd I tell you?" Helena answered, still stroking my cock.

There was a sudden silence. I listened carefully, and heard the soft sound of lips and tongues exploring each other. I was tempted to pull of the blindfold to watch.

There was a good deal of shuffling and moving of bodies. I went were I was nudged and positioned, happy to oblige, gently maneuvered off the mattress.

Soft hands – Marie's, I guessed correctly – moved me into place at the edge of the bed.

"Right here, Trump," she whispered, guiding me forward.

I reached out and felt a thigh stuck in the air. Helena was laying on her back, her pussy right there on the edge of the bed. Marie stood beside me.

I wasted no time, still overcome with lust. Helena was as soaked as I knew she'd be and I slid in without difficulty. I started out slow, barely restraining the impulse to fuck her with everything I had right from the start.

"That's it," Marie whispered in my ear. "Fuck her good, Trump, fuck her good."

Marie placed her hands on my shoulder, running her hands down my back as I fucked Helena.

"Come on, Trump," Marie urged me. "Fuck her hard. Nice and hard."

I sped up my pace and soon I was pounding Helena with vigor. Marie climbed in bed with her, still encouraging me.

"Fuck her hard, fuck her hard!" she kept shouting.

"That's it," Helena moaned. "Holy fuck, I'm gonna cum so fast!"

I felt a finger moving across Helena's clit. It moved from side to side rapidly, grazing my cock now and then. Helena howled and shrieked.

"That's it," Helena moaned. "Oh, fuck! Rub me harder, baby. Oh, fuck!"

That's when I realized the finger working Helena's clit was Marie's.

"That's it!" Marie said. "Give it to her, Trump."

I hammered her as hard as I could. Her shrieks turning into frenzied moans as I fucked her while Marie rubbed her clit. Helena became quiet, breathing-in deep and letting out a prolonged moan.

I knew by now the signs of Helena's orgasms and kept fucking her like a jackhammer. Her orgasm lasted a long time, Marie rubbing her clit hard throughout.

"Oh that felt so fucking good," Helena sighed.

I kept on fucking her, eager to come at last.

"Not yet, sweet Trump," Helena teased. "What kind of hostess would I be if I hogged your cock?"

Once again, bodies moved about and guided me into position. Only now it was Helena beside me. She led me onto the bed and guided my hands forward until they found Marie's ass. Marie was on her hands and knees again, this time waiting to be drilled from behind.

I placed my hands on Marie's butt cheeks and moved my cock into position. Marie reached back and guided me into her. Marie's pussy was still moist, almost as much as it was when she came a few minutes earlier.

I couldn't hold back anymore and started to fuck Marie at a decent pace right from the start. She responded, too, sighing loudly.

Helena stood behind me, kissing the back of my neck and nibbling it gently.

"You like that nice pussy, don't you?" Helena whispered in my ear. "Yeah, and that plump butt. I know you do. Fuck it good."

Helena slid her tongue into my ear. I thought I'd faint, the combination of sensations was so overwhelming. She wrapped her arms around my shoulders and whispered encouragement in my ears, kissing and nibbling my earlobes.

"That's it, fuck her!" she urged. "Fuck her! Fuck her!"

I couldn't hold back any further. I felt the first signs of a looming orgasm, the gentle tingle at the tip of my cock signaling its approach. Dimly, I was aware of Marie's second orgasm. She was in the final throes as my own loomed.

Scant moments later it arrived. I froze mid-thrust and pushed my cock into Marie as deeply as I could. The first throbs of my cock were like a joyous release, my lust pouring out from my cock as the waves of bliss and release swept through me.

The throbbing of my cock was as powerful as any orgasm I'd ever had. My cock throbbed ten or fifteen times in rapid, violent fashion before the surges of pleasure started to wane. Each successive pulsation was a little less powerful than the prior until, at long last, the final barely-perceptible twitch passed into memory.

I slid out of Marie and collapsed on the bed. I lay on my back, covered in sweat and breathing hard. I'd done a ten minute long sprint with hardly a breath.

The ladies settled into either side of me, snuggling close. I put an arm around their shoulders and pulled them tight. They each kissed me in turn, the warm sensuous kisses of the sexually spent.

***

I woke with a start, not remembering where I was for a moment. Then I recalled everything, peeling off the blindfold. I got out of bed, still naked.

I'd drifted off to sleep in a state of utter satisfaction, Helena and Marie in my arms. They must've slid out of bed quietly, probably chuckling at the young man half their age snoozing blissfully after they'd worn him out.

It didn't feel like I'd been asleep long, however. Shaking off the last of my nap, I got dressed. I heard a car door shutting as I stepped into the hall, crossed through the master bedroom, and looked out the front window.

A silver Audi was backing out of the driveway into the street. It drove away across my field of vision and I caught a glimpse of a dark-haired woman at the wheel.

"Goodbye Marie," I said, smiling.

Helena was downstairs in the kitchen pouring herself a glass of orange juice. She turned and smiled at me.

"Up so soon?" she said. "I thought we might've worn you out more than that."

"You wore me out plenty."

"I'm sure. You just missed Marie. Juice?"

"Sure," I said. "I saw her drive off, actually. Who was she?"

"Well, her name wasn't Marie." Helena poured me a glass and handed it to me. "That's her middle name. You met her, actually, yesterday when we were leaving the restaurant."

"Hannah and Kate?" My eyes grew wide. "Which one was it?"

"That I'm not going to tell you." She cast me one of her smirks. "I want you to always wonder."

I chuckled, thinking back to the encounter outside the café. I knew at once which it was, but said nothing.

"Well that was a dream come true," I said. "Thank you so much."

I took a long sip of juice and sat down at the island. Helena sat next to me. With a glance she read my somber thoughts.

"That wasn't your first time, was it?" I asked. "With Marie, I mean.

"I suppose that was obvious, huh?" Helena said. "I've joined her and her husband a few times that way and he owed me. They're an open couple and he was cool with it. It excites him, actually, the thought of his wife helping reward a deserving young man such as yourself. He'll probably fuck the shit out of her the second she gets home. Her pussy will be sore tomorrow. I know I won't be walking straight for a day or two after a weekend like this."

"You're like no one I've ever met," I observed. "You're so open about sex, so easygoing. Don't misunderstand me, I think it's great. Only it's, I don't know, a rarity."

"I've always been very sexual." She shrugged. "I don't believe there's anything wrong with that, either. It's natural, and it's who I am, and I make no apologies."

"Nor should you." I sighed. "Damn, I wish this weekend would never end."

"It doesn't have to, you know," Helena said. "In a manner of speaking."

"What'd you have in mind?" I asked. I'd wanted to broach the subject of where this was all going but was waiting for the right time.

"Nothing specific," Helena said. "Perhaps a weekly rendezvous?"

"I like the sound of that."

"Your apartment's on my way home, you know. It would be convenient to drop by and see my secret young stud."

"My roommate always works Thursday nights," I suggested.

"Well, there you go! But you'd have to promise me one thing."

"What's that?"

"How do I say this?" She paused, choosing her words carefully. "You have to promise me you won't let our arrangement stop you from other opportunities. After all, don't think it will restrict me in whatever arrangements I might have."

"For now," she continued. "Let's leave it about sex and have fun. I'll be your lover and your friend and your confidante, Trump, however long you want me in any combination of those capacities."

"Helena," I said. "That's some offer. I don't know what to say."

Helena smiled, her eyes lighting up.

"Trump, Sweet Trump," she sighed. "Don't you know how special you are? I'd never turn you away, not after what you did for me, and I'll be proud to be whatever I can be for you. You don't have to decide anything soon. Do you think you can handle that?"

"I do."

***

Gina welcomed me the next morning as I strode into work. She looked great, her dark eyes flashing at me as I walked in.

"Hey, you!" she said. "How was your weekend with your friend?"

"Great."

I stopped, a broad smile on my face.

"What are you up to tonight?" I asked.

"Nada." Gina smiled and our eyes met. "How come?"

"How about dinner?"

"That sounds nice."

"Right after work good?"

"Sure."

I settled into my work, considering my crowded calendar for the week ahead. I'd go out with Gina that night and Helena was coming over Thursday. Who knew where things would lead with either lady or what the future might hold. The possibilities were endless.

I was beginning to wonder if I was the luckiest bastard in the world.

Make America cum again.

1

Made in the USA
Coppell, TX
27 December 2022